AF464691

SAM DOWLING

Is a Dublin-born playwright. He has written and produced nearly thirty plays or small-cast versions of classics for Praxis Theatre Laboratory. His subject-matter has ranged from Irish history through the lives of writers and artists to re-working of themes from the Greek myths. His play about the Brontës (co-written with Andrea Bird) has had three productions in Tokyo.
For more detail see listing in playwrights' database at www.doollee.com

PRAXIS THEATRE LABORATORY is an experimental theatre which seeks its direction from the actors' response to the work. No-one takes on a separate role as director. We particularly value images conjured in rehearsal, and intuitive and emotional rather than intellectual or technical evaluation. We try to fix as little as possible and each performance retains an element of improvisation.
Founded by Sam Dowling as the in-house company at The Tabard in West London from 1984, in 1990 we left to pursue more experimental goals. We opened a small theatre space in County Roscommon, Ireland in 1999 and have toured UK, USA, Ireland, Belgium, Netherlands, Ukraine and Poland.

IRISH PLAYS AND OTHERS BY SAM DOWLING
IN PRINT OR IN THE PIPELINE

RIVERMAN [Walter Greaves, naïf painter, rise and fall.]
CAULDRON OF BRONTËS [Genius siblings.]
A SEASON IN HELL [Wild poets Rimbaud and Verlaine.]
MOUNTAIN [Life-changing encounters]
RENEWAL [Site-specific version of MOUNTAIN]
TROJAN WOMEN
BIRTH OF THE BEAST [Northern Ireland.]
BIG FELLA! [Michael Collins.]
ALLEGIANCE [IRA in London.]
ANTIGONE
THE FLAME AND THE STONE [Yeats and Maud Gonne.]
VIRGIN OF NOTTING HILL [Sexual problems.]
ORESTEIAN TRILOGY
LOVELOST [Abuse]
RED COUNTESS GREEN CROW [Markievicz and O'Casey]
HA! HA! HA! [Improvisations on Coward and Shakespeare.]

AND SMALL-CAST VERSIONS OF THESE CLASSICS;

THE CENCI
IMPORTANCE OF BEING EARNEST
CHERRY ORCHARD
THREE SISTERS
HEDDA GABLER
WHEN WE DEAD AWAKEN
HAMLET
MACBETH
ANTONY AND CLEOPATRA
THE TEMPEST

A SEASON IN HELL was first performed at the Tabard Theatre in west London in 1989 with this cast:

RIMBAUD..Herman Stephens
VERLAINE..Phil O'Sullivan
MOTHER..Pia Ditley
FIFI...Pia Ditley

Designed by Paul Dowling

For performing permission and terms contact Sam Dowling

IRISH PLAYS AND OTHERS Volume 11

A SEASON IN HELL

a play by Sam Dowling

Sam Dowling
85 Haddo House
Haddo Street
London SE10 9SE

e-mail praxis.lab@ntlworld.com

Published by Lulu 2007

www.lulu.com

ISBN 978-1-84753-888-8

A SEASON IN HELL

THE CHARACTERS
in
A SEASON IN HELL

THE MOTHER....................................Verlaine's mother

PAUL VERLAINE ....a poet

ARTHUR RIMBAUD......................... a poet

FIFI.. a whore

A SEASON IN HELL
by Sam Dowling

PART ONE

'BLACK'

[All the actors remain on stage throughout the performance. In the Ukraine tour, we had the MOTHER up on a high pedestal which was covered by her enormously long dress.

MOTHER and VERLAINE create an image which may reflect Birth and Oppression.]

FIFI

'A noir, E blanc, I rouge, U vert, O Bleu: voyelles
Je dirai quelque jour vos naissances latentes...'

MOTHER

Are you finished ?

[VERLAINE crawls away. MOTHER, in black, talking to a foetus she keeps in a large glass jar. She puts the finishing touches to her very bourgeois appearance.]

One day I shall reveal your secret birth
....
Tch ! Only black sets off my...
Manners ! Decorum ! Intelligent conversation !
I should imagine M. Rimbaud to be... very grand...handsome in a remote kind of way
Totally *distingué*

[DOORBELL OFF]

Oh ! Oh my ! Do I look a mess ?
Off to sleepy-byes now my darling...

[Enter RIMBAUD, a lanky dishevelled youth with dirty hair, wearing homemade clothes far too small for him, perhaps a dirty piece of string for a necktie and a peasant's cap. He is grinning happily.]

RIMBAUD
Howaya missus ?

MOTHER
What are you doing up here boy ?

RIMBAUD
Arthur Rimbaud missus
Come to stay with Verlaine the poet

MOTHER
Aagh
How do you....?
Won't you... eh?
Aaagh

RIMBAUD
Not a bad day that...after the rain

MOTHER
Rain ?
Paul... M. Verlaine met you at The Gard de L'Est ?

RIMBAUD
No one at the station but yer man for the tickets
Last time I come to Paris
I did a two-week stretch in Mazas prison for travelling without a ticket

MOTHER
Ooagh !

RIMBAUD
Verlaine sent me the money this time

MOTHER

There is a very strange smell...
Eh... Did you have any difficulty finding a cab, Monsieur eh... ?

RIMBAUD

I don't have no money for cabs Missus

MOTHER

No
Perhaps you would like to eh wash and change after your long journey from...the Provinces ?

RIMBAUD

I'm wearing every blessed stitch I've got

MOTHER

The new shops on the Champs Elysees are quite the rage
Expensive but as my father always said
'Quality is no extravagance '

RIMBAUD

Verlaine wrote me a beautiful invitation
'Come great beloved soul I call to you
I await your coming !'

MOTHER

And forgot to meet your train
How droll
Probably he has entirely forgotten you exist
He leads a very full life

[ENTER VERLAINE, breathless.]

VERLAINE

He wasn't on the train
I waited till....

MOTHER

Paul

RIMBAUD
Master Verlaine

VERLAINE
Oh
Rimbaud !
....
'Come great beloved soul I call to you
I await your coming !' Ha ha ha ha !

[Instant rapport between the two men.
They clasp hands passionately.]

Did you finish the long poem ?

RIMBAUD
Yes

VERLAINE
You brought it ?

RIMBAUD
Oh yes

VERLAINE
Where is it for heaven's sake ?

[RIMBAUD fishes out some dog-eared sheets.]

May I ?

MOTHER
'Clothes maketh the man' my father always said
His fortune came from oil
Culinary oil
Naturally there was a great deal of land
Land is the prerequisite for good breeding
Outside Paris

RIMBAUD
My mother plotted all her life
To get her paws on a few acres of land
Her brother was pissing up against the wall of the local pub

MOTHER
Well !

RIMBAUD
She got it in the end
Had him certified after one unholy binge

MOTHER
Ahem !
The family has a firm tradition of public service
My son Paul insisted on taking a position in The City Hall
Though I would have been perfectly content to see him devote
Every waking moment to his...muse
One's hope is that [MOTHER indicates the foetus] one of the younger boys
Will follow their Papa into a military career
He took a commission in the Engineers

RIMBAUD
I was buggered by an entire troop of Engineers
Last time I was in Paris

MOTHER
Really !
Paul !

RIMBAUD
When they finished they stood around
And spat tobacco juice ever me like I was a spitoon

MOTHER
I shan't listen to this filth !

RIMBAUD
I'm just saying what I know about the Army

MOTHER
Officer class you stupid vicious child !
Officer class !

RIMBAUD
I always say 'I haven't been in the Army
But the Army's been in me '
Officers and all missus

MOTHER
I trust you will have no difficulty in finding somewhere to stay
In Paris M.Rimbaud

VERLAINE
He's staying here love

MOTHER
Paul...

VERLAINE
Good night my darling

[Kisses her passionately.]

MOTHER
See the silver is all locked away before you retire Paul

VERLAINE
....Rimbaud you have broken every rule
And written the most extraordinary poem !

RIMBAUD
You like it

VERLAINE
Some echoes of... I don't know what

RIMBAUD
It owes a lot to you

VERLAINE
Far beyond anything I've written
....
Baudelaire !

RIMBAUD
A starting point
Baudelaire is the great seer... the great savant
But he remains a slave to form to rhyme...to sin ! Ha ha ha 1
I've broken through all that
I am a sorcerer... a voyant

VERLAINE
A voyeur ?

RIMBAUD
If necessary yes

VERLAINE
I'll show you a thing or two young fellow !

RIMBAUD
So far... I'm only sixteen you know... it's been all imagination...

VERLAINE
No

RIMBAUD
Except childhood things
And the soldiers

VERLAINE
That's enough

RIMBAUD
It's not enough

[VERLAINE reading from Le Bateau d'Ivre.
Perhaps FIFI recites it concurrently in French,
Or the script is shown in projection.]

VERLAINE
'I have seen the setting sun shit upon by alien monsters
Lit up with long purple scabs
Like actors in a play of long long ago
The distant waves rolling their trembling shutters...'

FIFI
*'J'ai vu le soliel bas, taché d'horreurs mystiques
Illuminant de longs figements violets
Pareils à des acteurs de drames très antiques
Les flots roulant au loin leurs frissons de volets...'*

VERLAINE
The images are so chaotic but...

RIMBAUD
They work !

VERLAINE
They work !
......
Astonishing ! What do you call it ?

RIMBAUD
Le Bateau d'Ivre

VERLAINE
You make poetry here of... a child shitting in the yard

RIMBAUD
Of course

[Again, concurrently FIFI may recite.]

VERLAINE

'If I long for any water of Europe, it is that
Cold black pool where, in the embalmed evening light
A squatting child, full of sadnesses, releases
A boat, frail as a May butterfly....'
......
Oh my God, Rimbaud !

FIFI

'Si je désire une eau d'Europe, c'est la flache
Noire et froid où vers le crépuscule embaumé
Un enfant accroupi plein de tristesses, lache
Un bateau frêle comme un papillon de mai....'

RIMBAUD

You must teach me everything

VERLAINE

I have nothing to teach you

RIMBAUD

Life ! The city ! Women !
Can you get drugs ?

VERLAINE

I can get hashish

RIMBAUD

I smoke a lot of tobacco when I can get it
I know a bit about alcohol

VERLAINE

Absinthe ?

RIMBAUD

Beer and brandy

VELAINE
Absinthe is the Queen of Paris
I shall present you at her court this very night !

RIMBAUD
At her cunt ?

VERLAINE
That too Rimbaud that too !

RIMBAUD
Good
....
This... your mother's house ?

VERLAINE
I have no rent to pay

RIBAUD
I hate the bourgeoisie

VERLAINE
I have a very young wife

RIMBAUD
What rotten luck

VERLAINE
My mother pays all the bills

RIMBAUD
My mother treats me like a criminal
Some night I'll go back and cut her throat

VERLAINE
We've had a child

RIMBAUD
What ever for ?

VERLAINE
I like children

RIMBAUD
I would exterminate half the human race by slow torture
As a matter of principle
The bourgeosie would head the queue believe me
Are you a Communard ?

VERLAINE
The National Guard
I'm still sort-of on the run
We had to move house when the Commune fell
Daren't go back to my job at the City Hall
[Shouting suddenly] REACTIONARY SWINE !!

RIMBAUD
The Commune was the opportunity of the millennium

VERLAINE
Yes

RIMBAUD
Listen
I believe passionately we must put the axe to the very roots of society
Church, family government... the gutter press of course, except ours !
Ha ha ha !

VERLAINE
Exactly ! Ha ha ha !

RIMBAUD
You fought at the barricades ?

VELAINE
What would you think ?   [Takes a bullet from pocket.]
A souvenir: this one had my name on it...
Missed my head by a hair's breadth

RIMBAUD
God I envy you

VERLAINE
.....
Actually... in the Commune...when the fighting started
I....I hid myself in the broom cupboard

RIMBAUD
You should be executed

VERLAINE
In the broom cupboard with the maid to protect me
I ignored the mobilisation call
Refused to join my comrades
I am the most despicable coward Rimbaud !
...
My mother was missing for the best part of a week
On the barricades with the riff-raff of Paris as it turned out
I was worried sick needless to say
But too terrified to go out looking for her... there were bodies all over the place...
Eventually I picked up enough courage to... to send my wife out looking for her
My wife was y'know pregnant... she's only nineteen...
....
Three days and night she spent searching among the corpses
I can't tell you how painful it was for me... alone except for the maid
As I said when the fighting came down this way
I locked myself in the broom cupboard with the maid

RIMBAUD
With the maid

VERLAINE
We barricaded ourselves in with... with mattresses actually....
There was nothing funny about it believe me !

RIMBAUD
And the bullet ?

VERLAINE
My wife
Someone took a potshot at her
Hit the doorpost by her head
Burned her fingers when she picked it up
I had three days in that hell-hole !
My wife and mother arrived home within half an hour of each other when the fighting stopped
They took me out and we... we had breakfast on the balcony
Mother had got hold of fresh croissants... don't ask me where or how
We had coffee and croissants on the balcony and watched Paris burning
It had a certain beauty...
Like Nero
Except I had no fiddle
....
I don't feel ashamed

RIMBAUD
How many times did you screw her... in the cupboard ?

VERLAINE
I wept a lot
She held me like a child

RIMBAUD
.....
Take me to a brothel

VERLAINE
Eh ? Oh sure

RIMBAUD
Now

VERLAINE
Feeling randy are we ? Ha ha ha !

RIMBAUD
Will you help me do it properly ?

VERLAINE
I'll put it in for you
Like a stallion

RIMBAUD
I have no money

VERLAINE
Mother pays for everything
We'll have a few snorts of absinthe first and ....

RIMBAUD
Can she afford to debauch me ?

VERLAINE
I can twist her round that little finger 1
Anything ! Simply anything I demand !
I'm going to take you to the Café Cluny first....
'Literary Paris !' All the Parnassians are dying to meet you
You'll be like Christ among the doctors
They're expecting a middle-aged pompous old bore like themselves !
Venez *chere grande âme*
On vous appelle on vous attende ! Ha ha ha ha !

PART TWO

'WHITE'

[The two men in search of their brothel.]

RIMBAUD
White is the colour of pure poetry

VERLAINE
Wear this

RIMBAUD
'Purity of white mists, tents, virgin kings
Fierce spears of glaciers, trembling pistils of flowers...'

VERLAINE
You must be properly dressed for losing your virginity

RIMBAUD
Finding the road to hell

VERLAINE
You'll have to hurry to catch up with me ! Ha ha ha !

RIMBAUD
I'm deadly serious

VERLAINE
No place on that road for a sour-puss... or a pauper

RIMBAUD
My pockets have huge holes in them
So I can masturbate in front of my mother

VERLAINE
Tch ! The foolish virgin

RIMBAUD

I am preparing for the diabolical bridegroom

VERLAINE
You have the eyes of a seraph, the face of an angel... and the mouth of a jackal

RIMBAUD
To Hell if you please !

VELAINE
Choosing one's brothel is a delicate process
One's brothel must precisely evoke the mood of the moment...

RIMBAUD
Desperation

VERLAINE
Exquisite anticipation

RIMBAUD
I must degrade myself

VERLAINE
Hmm... Madame Fifi's place perhaps...
She will put you through the entire gamut of degradation for five francs
You will be amazed

RIMBAUD
I will be a poet

VERLAINE
You are that

RIMBAUD
I think I am
No... It's wrong to say 'I think'
The poet is no more than the instrument expressing The Unknown as it awakes in mankind

'Mankind thinks me'

VERLAINE
Verlaine thinks you a bit deranged

RIMBAUD
Yes
I shall leap through unheard undreamt of horrors
Purging myself of all kinds of love all kinds of suffering all kinds of madness...
But holding on to their quintessence like the sorcerer I am becoming...
Unspeakable tortures where I shall need all my faith all my superhuman strength...
Can you come that road with me Verlaine ?

VERLAINE
I like my comforts

RIMBAUD
We shall become the great madmen the great criminals the supreme scholars
Because we shall reach the Unnameable the Unknown !

VERLAINE
Merat says my poetry is the apotheosis of the bourgeois dream

RIMBAUD
I forgive you because I love you
And we shall enter Hell together and become the true thieves of fire!

VERLAINE
The Parnassian poets...

RIMBAUD
Are eaters of shit !
You are already way beyond them
You and Merat are the only poets in the entire bunch
Anyway since the Greeks poetry has been a joke

VERLAINE
Racine a joke ?

RIMBAUD
I concede Racine

VERLAINE
Baudelaire a joke ?

RIMBAUD
Baudelaire was true god... but he lost his balls at the final rampart
He is afraid of Jesus Christ
We are gong to beat God at his own game
We shall appropriate the Second Coming !
We shall bring hope to the second millennium !

VERLAINE
Some hope !

RIMBAUD
YES ! SOME HOPE AT LAST !
IT'S YOU AND ME OR ANOTHER TWO THOUSAND YEARS OF SEWAGE !

VERLAINE
We start where Racine left off

RIMBAUD
Where the Greeks left off

VERLAINE
Harmony

[Pehaps we hear FIFI recite
Verlaine's L'HEURE EXQUISE]

RIMBAUD
Harmony

VERLAINE
I venture to say there's some of it in my work already

RIMBAUD
That's why I came to Paris

FIFI
'La lune blanche
Luit dans les bois:
De chaque branche
Part une voix
Sous la ramée...'

A bien-aimée.

Un vaste et tendre
Apaisment
Semble descendre
Du firmament
Que l'astre irise...

C'est l'heure exquise.'

VERLAINE
'White moon
Through trees;
A voice calls
From the underskirt
Of every branch...

O my beloved

Aurora of tender
Harmony
Dropping
From a rainbow
Firmament of stars...

This is the exquisite hour.'

[Dance music and coarse laughter
from within as Madame FIFI
offers her wares to passers-by.]

FIFI

Bon soir Mesieurs !
Come in for a short time, sonny !
Bring in your father for a fiddle of fun from me ten topless bottomless beauty-of-Bath belles of yer balls !
Every last one a virgin and nothing in the house over five francs !
Good clean family fun !
Come in and have a gander up the goose of the Queen of Sheba !
She won't bite yah ! Unless you pay her extra ! Ha ha ha !
You're only makin it hard for yourself standing out there like two spare priests at a christening !
Quatre francs vin et service compris !
Bring in your son mister and we'll show him what it's for

VERLAINE

Hello Fifi !

FIFI

Oh bon soir M. Verlaine...Ca va ?

VERLAINE

Two for five francs Fifi ?

RIMBAUD

She's nauseating

FIFI

Watch yer fucking language yeh snivelling cat's melt of a country cretin !
Will yah look at the cut of him ?
You needn't think you're trampin over my Axminster in them clogs !
I'll have no louse-ridden tip of a dungheap snuff-diving on my anti-Macassar
Belfast linen panjandrams and me laundryman on his long weekend off !

Three francs for yourself M. Verlaine
Five plus laundry for the bogman !

RIMBAUD
She reminds me of my puritan mother

VERLAINE
Six for the pair of us Fifi
It's all I've got

[FIFI and VERLAINE sing and dance wildly.]

FIFI & VERLAINE [sing]
Danson la gigue !
Danson la gigue !
J'aimais surtout ses jolis yeux
Plus clairs que l'étoile des cieux
J'aimais ses yeux malicieux

Dansons la gigue !

[RIMBAUD tries to drag them apart.]

RIMBAUD
I WANT MORE DRINK !

FIFI
PISS OFF YAH STINKIN TURD ! PISS OFF !

[A drunken fracas ensues.
Sound of POLICE WHISTLES.
FIFI makes a tactical withdrawal.]

VERLAINE
Dansons la gigue....

[RIMBAUD and VERLAINE dance a little.
They look as if they might kiss.]

VERLAINE
Rimbe...

[VERLAINE passes out.
RIMBAUD stands over him.]

RIMBAUD
Jig me a jig
The best I found was this
Kiss of a flowering mouth
Then she was...dead

[RIMBAUD falls across his friend's body.
DAWN. The two men awaken in the gutter.]

VERLAINE
Dansons la gigue
Oh God my head
Oh God my head

RIMBAUD
Is there a bar open at this hour ?

VERLAINE
Round the corner
Left

RIMBAUD
My mouth tastes like a whore's crutch

VERLAINE
You make me feel so....
I have this extraordinary energy
I must write
Do you mind if I go home ?

RIMBAUD
Let's work together

VERLAINE
Oh yes it must be with you

RIMBAUD

We'll get a few drinks inside us...
When the sun is up we'll go into the Bois de Bouloigne and...
Have you any paper ?

VERLAINE
Work at my place

RIMBAUD
Your women hate me

VERLAINE
Oh ?
I'll get paper at the Café Cluny
Yes mother thinks you're after my ring
Mt wife says you're turning me against her and the child

RIMBAUD
A poet has no business trying to be respectable

VERLAINE
I tried to kill them the other night actually
Absinthe does funny things to my equilibrium
Threw the child at the bloody wall
Tried to set fire to the wife's hair

RIMBAUD
You're lying again

VERLAINE
She didn't even resist
Sat there staring dumbly at me
Her fucking hair won't burn

RIMBAUD
You haven't the guts

VERLAINE
I'm always running out of matches
When I sobered up... in the morning

She insisted we make love

RIMBAUD
Love ?
You call that love ?

VERLAINE
Oh yes a perfect family in many respects

RIMBAUD
At home... in Charleville...
I used to lure stray bitches back to our yard and fuck them

VERLAINE
No need to invent things for me

RIMBAUD
Let's find a couple of strays

VERLAINE
You were afraid to come into the brothel

RIMBAUD
There's a cat ! Psssswssh !

VERLAINE
You're afraid of women
Well I'm not

RIMBAUD
Psswshwsshwssss !

VERLAINE
Poor Rimbe !
Come... we'll drown it in absinthe

RIMBAUD
I want hashish

VERLAINE
We haven't the money for hashish

RIMBAUD
Go home and get it Master Verlaine
Go home to your Mama and get it !

VERLAINE
If I go home they won't let me out again

RIMBAUD
What a miserable shit you are

VERLAINE
They love me
Really love me

RIMBAUD
Love has to be re-invented obviously
Now all that women want is security
Once they have that
Heart and beauty are set aside

VERLAINE
I accept people as they are

RIMBAUD
Sometimes I can see beyond what they are
Slaves of slaves
To what they might become
The woman poet will exist but only when she lives for and by herself
When we men release her from her chains
'Virtue'...' Motherhood' All that crap
Then she will find strange unfathomable things
Repulsive delicious things that we cannot reach
But we'll accept them from her hands
And understand her poetry
....
Now will you go and get that money Paul

VERLAINE
I'll be back in half an hour
Get yourself a coffee
And don't move out of sight of that corner

[VERLAINE discovered in post-prandial langour
being petted or entertained by his mother.]

VERLAINE
Don't stop !

MOTHER
Paul I want you to talk to the Debussey child about your work

VERLAINE
I feel deliciously spoiled this evening

MOTHER
He says it's pure magic

VERLAINE
So it is

MOTHER
He's only eleven

VERLAINE
'Out of the mouths of babes and sucklings...'

MOTHER
He was singing your *'Clair de Lune'* this morning
To a little tune he composed himself

VERLAINE
That Debussey brat has taste if not talent

MOTHER
He's a prodigy

VERLAINE
Mother !

MOTHER
I hope I'm not getting arthritis
My fingers are quite stiff

VERLAINE
Let me...
I saw you washing clothes the other morning
That's servants' work

MOTHER
I can't bear anyone else touching your things... even Mathilde

VERLAINE
Never forgave me for coming out of napkins did you ?

MOTHER
I love babies... of all ages ! Ha ha ha !
.....
Happy to be with your old mother again Paul ?

VERLAINE
The prodigal poet !
'Happy' hardly describes it

MOTHER
I have a superb brace of pheasant for tomorrow

VERLAINE
The fatted calf !

MOTHER
We have to build you up again

VERLAINE
....

Any of that claret left... for the pheasant ?

MOTHER
It hasn't been touched since you...

VERLAINE
Celery
Braise them with celery and that cream sauce of yours

MOTHER
And the claret

VERLAINE
Oh mother !

MOTHER
....
Mathilde wrote...
She's so pleased you haven't gone back to the cretin

VERLAINE
Let's take a cab and bring them home tonight !
I mean I have the right !

MOTHER
She promised if you're good for another couple of days
They'll come at the weekend

VERLAINE
Mathilde and I... I've never known two people so perfectly matched
You must never let her forget how profoundly I love them both
I haven't wavered from that even when I....

MOTHER
She gets frightened when you drink that terrible absinthe
So do I

VERLAINE
'Absinthe makes the heart grow fonder !' Ha ha ha !

MOTHER
I'm serious

VERLAINE
Absinthe releases some kind of anarchy in me
Like a thousand little demons
At best it can be quite creative

MOTHER
I live in dread of anarchy in this house

VERLAINE
All art is controlled anarchy

MOTHER
Anarchy is uncontrollable
Like the Commune
You know what that did to you

VERLAINE
I wasn't ready for it
After Rimbaud....

MOTHER
Let's not talk about that

VERLAINE
In the Commune you and Mathilde somehow contained the chaos
Like in the womb
......
You know I have perfectly lucid memories
Of my time in your womb Mother
You didn't drink in those days did you ?

MOTHER
Never

VERLAINE
I still feel that intoxication when we're together like this
Apart from the way you feed me
....
The oceanic warmth of your love

MOTHER
What a delightful phrase
'The oceanic warmth of a mother's love'
You might use it in a poem one day

VERLAINE
If I ever write another poem

MOTHER
Wait and see what wonderful work you'll do
With your little family around you
Mathilde inspired your very best poetry I always think...
La Bonne Chanson...

VERLAINE
Rimbaud might have made a real poet of me

MOTHER
Tch !

VERLAINE
Poetry is a dangerous game Mother !
I have a soft underbelly
Can't take the punishment

MOTHER
Well thank God for that
I try never to criticise my sons but...

VERLAINE
<u>You have only one son Mother !</u>

MOTHER
Made it a rule
Always accept them as they are and love them

VERLAINE
You could at least keep that thing... in the larder or somewhere
Out of my sight
'In a cool place'...like strawberry jam

MOTHER
Perfectly content to potter around the house with me...
He's excellent with the servants

VERLAINE
My consolation is that all the family morbidity is screwed into that bottle

MOTHER
Your obsession with the pornographic cretin is essentially morbid

VERLAINE
Pornography is all to do with intentions
Rimbaud is never pornographic
Erotic certainly
But his intentions are depressingly serious
Religious one might say

MOTHER
Oh certainly not religious

VERLAINE
He is constantly searching for God

MOTHER
No sane man searches for God in the bawdy-houses of Montmartre

VERLAINE
Oh yes they do
And even in Hell Mother

MOTHER
That's blasphemous !
And anyway it's a blatant contradiction
Hell is the absence of God

VERLAINE
You've forgotten your Catechism
'God is everywhere'
How or why should hell be the exception ?

MOTHER
Oh ! Ha ha ha ha ha ! I think that's a really nice point
If God is omnipresent he must be in Hell ! Ha ha ha !
I shall put it to Father Laclerc next time he calls !
What clever sons I have ! Ha ha ha !

[RIMBAUD, dirtier and emaciated after
several weeks living rough, shuffling
about in the street near Verlaine's home.
The other passing briskly.]

VERLAINE
Oh my God ! Rimbaud !

RIMBAUD
What do you want with me ?

VERLAINE
I've searched Paris for weeks
Where the devil have you been ?

RIMBAUD
Here and there
Money ?

VERLAINE
Of course

RIMBAUD
Money !

VERLAINE
Where are you living ?

RIMBAUD
Money !!

VERLAINE
You look like death

RIMBAUD
You look like a seminarian's gigolo

VEERLAINE
Let me get you some clothes
Take you to my...

RIMBAUD
You promised to take me to Hell
I expect your Mammy wouldn't let you
Or your wife

VERLAINE
We're very content

RIMBAUD
Disgusting !
Still beating your son's head off the wall ?
The wife's hair burning any better ?

VERLAINE
Oh your poor beautiful face !

RIMBAUD
Traitor !

VERLAINE
I am irresistibly drawn back into the womb of bourgeois family life
You've no idea how safe and warm it is

RIMBAUD
[Spits.]

VERLAINE
I haven't written an honest word since I lost sight of you

RIMBAUD
....
I haven't written a word since you dumped me

VERLAINE
I am so easily led Rimbe

RIMBAUD
Have you killed your mother yet ?

VERLAINE
Have you killed yours ?

[BOTH laugh]

I can feel that energy rising

RIMBAUD
Yes

VERLAINE
Let's go on the rampage ! Now !

RIMBAUD
And work ?

VERLAINE
Everything !
We'll get a room in a doss-house and...

RIMBAUD
Come on then !

VERLAINE
Oh my God what a stink ! Ha ha ha ha ha !

FIFI [Sings]
Who dares to love me ?
They say I am a whore
Who dares to love me ?
My crutch an open sewer
Who dares to love me ?
My heart is turned to stone
Who dares to love me must join my dream or walk alone oh !

Who dares to love me ?
I prowl the empty streets
Who dares to love me
Where dead and dying meet ?
Who dares to love me
Against the alley wall ?
Who dares to love me must cry the vampire's lonely call oh !

Who dares to love me
In the forests of the night ?
Who dares to love me
And suck the dragon's bite ?
Who dares to love me
A werewolf in my womb ?
Who dares to love me your body mating with the moon oh !?

Lightning crashing on the moon oh !
Lightning flashing on the moon oh !
Lightning....lightning....lightning....lightning....light....

[RIMBAUD has been discarding
his lice-ridden clothes and will dress in clean.]

VERLAINE
What am I supposed to do with this filth ?

RIMBAUD
They won't bite you

VERLAINE
They bit you
....
....
Dear beauteous body....

RIMBAUD
Write this for me please....
'Tall against a backdrop of snow a being of beauty. Wind-whispers of death and waves of soft music rise up, swell and tremble like a ghost, this worshipped body...'

VERLAINE
This worshipped body...

RIMBAUD
'Scarlet and black wounds throbbing through proud flesh. The colours of life itself deepen, dance an aura about the vision before us. And the tremblings, rising and threatening, and the strange taste of these effects'

VERLAINE
Taste of these effects...

RIMBAUD
'And the whispering wind of life and the raucous music of reality, left far behind, impaled on our mother of beauty,--- she recoils, stands erect. Oh !'

VERLAINE
Oh !

RIMBAUD

' Our bones are reclothed in a new living body.
Oh ashen-face, scraggy-haired escutcheon, crystal arms !
Cannon on which I must throw myself through the melee of trees and lightest air !'

VERLAINE

Cannon on which I must throw myself through the melee of trees and lightest air !

PART THREE

'RED'

[FIFI may recite in French.]

RIMBAUD
'Purples, spit blood, laughter of lovely lips
Enraged or in he drunkard's whining penitence...'

FIFI
'Pourpes, sang craché, rire des levres belle
Dans la colere ou les ivresses penitentes...'

VERLAINE
You debase everything I do

RIMBAUD
You do

VERLAINE
Rimbe !

RIMBAUD
You never stop whining

VERLAINE
I have never written so well been so happy so productive

RIMBAUD
I nearly taught you objectivity

VERLAINE
I'm too emotional to be objective
....
You split my lip last night

RIMBAUD
It's pissing rain

VERLAINE
All I ask is..if not love...at least understanding

RIMBAUD
The rain pisses gently on the town

VERLAINE
...
May I read you something ?

RIMBAUD
If you must

[Again FIFI may join in]

VERLAINE
'Tears fall in my heart
As soft rain on the town
What is this ennui
That seeps through my heart ?

O soft din of the rain
On the earth on the on the roofs
For the yearning heart
O the poem of the rain !

Senseless tears
In the self-rejecting heart
What ! No hint of betrayal ?
Senseless anguish !
For sure the worst pain
Is not knowing why
Without love without hate
My heart is so full of pain '

FIFI

'Il pleure dans mon coeur
Comme il pleut sur la ville,
Quelle est cette langueur
Qui pénètre mon coeur ?

O bruit doux de la pluie
Par terre et sur les toits !
Pour un coeur qui s'ennuie
O le chant de la pluie !

Il pleure sans raison
Dans le coeur qui s'écoeure.
Quoi ! Nulle trahison ?
Ce deuil est sans raison.
C'est bien la pire peine
De ne savoir pourquoi,
Sans amour et sans haine,
Mon coeur a tant de peine.'

RIMBAUD

God is beginning to speak through both of us
This is pure alchemy
The meaning and purpose of poetry
To know to become God
I...'I' am a piece of timber that has become a violin
A perfect instrument upon which God plays the secret music of the universe
.....
Soon... I believe this Verlaine... I shall take the instrument from God's hands
And I shall play it
I shall be God !
And I shall bring together good and evil
Cold and warmth prayer and debauch
That is my great work on earth !
I ad the strictest Christian upbringing you know
It's not easy for me to embrace sin and degradation
My whole psyche recoils from it

VERLAINE
Mine leads me to relish it to the last dreg !

RIMBAUD
I worry about your disposition

VERLAINE
I am every day fatally torn between my family and our art

RIMBAUD
I opened your eyes
If you don't want to see that's your affair

VERLAINE
I was a poet before you turned up on my doorstep

RIMBAUD
You had the makings of a poet
You still have if you pay the price

VERLAINE
Try to understand the love in my family

RIMBAUD
Tch !

VERLAINE
Mother and me... the wife...even the child

RIMBAUD
Quit it, will you ?

VERLAINE
Don't try to tell me love is incompatible with poetry

RIMBAUD
.....
There was a girl...I wrote to her and arranged a...

An assignation in the wood by the river
I was nearly fourteen and ready for anything
I knew what was what...from watching our neighbour's dog at stud
A German Pointer
Anyway she arrives...the girl... with her great lump of a sister in tow
She was so beautiful
I couldn't speak
Not one fucking word could I get out... and they started to giggle
They went into convulsions
I turned and ran and ran and ran through the wood out into the fields
Till I fell into a ditch
I tried to drown myself in that ditch
There was only a couple of inches of water
I caught a really bad cold out of it

VERLAINE
Poor Rimbe !
I have no problem with women
I'm going to divide my time...a month with you...a month with my family and...

RIMBAUD
I'll murder you in your sleep if you attempt any such thing
I mean that !
...
Money !

VERLAINE
I have none

RIMBAUD
Have you written to the harridan ?

VERLAINE
You know damn well she won't cough up while I'm with you
That's why I...

RIMBAUD
Go there and get it off her...now

Use force if necessary
I'm going bloody sane for want of a drink !
If you stay overnight you needn't come back

VERLAINE
You have no human feelings !

RIMBAUD
ME ?   NO WHAT ?
I'M CARRYING THE FEELINGS OF THE ENTIRE HUMAN RACE IN MY FUCKING GORGE !
Now get out of here and don't come back without the money !
PIMP !

[MOTHER crooning to the foetus in its jar.]

MOTHER
'Dansons la gigue !
Je me souviens, je me souviens
Des heures et des entretiens
Et c'est le meilleur de mes biens...'

VERLAINE
Mother !

MOTHER
Oh my God ! Paul !

VERLAINE
I love you so much Mother

MOTHER
My baby ! My baby !

VERLAINE
Where are the others ?

MOTHER
Gone to a matineé

We've been so worried about you

VERAINE
I could do with a drink

MOTHER
I wish you wouldn't

VERLAINE
My tummy's a bit upset

MOTHER
You haven't been eating properly
You must remember your health Paul and look at that shirt !
Your room is full of clean clothes
Let me put you in a bath...

VERLAINE
I need some money

MOTHER
Of course
We'll go to the bank first thing in the morning

VERLAINE
We haven't eaten since..

MOTHER
Forgive me pet... I'll have something sent up right away

VERLAINE
I'll eat with Rimbaud if....

MOTHER
You're wife and child haven't seen you for a week
The girl is distraught and th...

VERLAINE
Don't start on me as soon as I'm in the door Mother !

MOTHER
I'm sorry

VERLAINE
Let me have some money and I'll be back to stay in a day or so

MOTHER
You're not going back to that creature he's a...

VERLAINE
STOP IT !

MOTHER
.....
.....
The children miss you

VERLAINE
What 'children' ?

[MOTHER anxiously polishes the foetus's jar.]

MOTHER
......

VERLAINE
Aw for heaven's sake !

MOTHEER
You should set an example
....
Your cousin Victor says he'll get him into the Chasseurs when he grows up

VERLAINE
Even the Army won't take in pickled abortions
The officers' mess is full of them already

MOTHER
Don't be cruel to us

VERLAINE
You have to face up to it sooner or later
He's not going to grow up !

MOTHER
Neither are you it seems

VERLAINE
....
Poor Mam...
.....
I need fifty francs

MOTHER
Tomorrow I'll give you five francs

VERLAINE
I wish to Christ I could go back to my job !

MOTHER
Everyone else has gone back to their jobs
There's nothing stopping you except your own laziness

VERLAINE
Half the poets in Paris are in gaol
Did you hear what they did to de Sivry ?
I couldn't take torture Mother !

MOTHER
Paul !

VERLAINE
There's thirty thousand Communards in chains
And God knows how many more in hiding !

MOTHER
I'll swear in any court you spent the days of the fighting in the linen-cupboard

VERLAINE
I'll cut my bloody throat before I let them take me !

MOTHER
Forgive me love

VERLAINE
I should have put an end to myself long since
I am anathema to every soul I loved and needed

MOTHER
Don't say that !

VERLAINE
You want me to beg for every crust that goes into my mouth

MOTHER
The larder is bursting with food
Let me ring f...

VERLAINE
My only friend is out there in a filthy hovel starving
And you want me to gorge myself in your rotten fleshpots !

MOTHER
He is the child of the Devil !

VERLAINE
You want to stuff me and turn me into some kind of specimen...
Sitting on your bloody mahogany table like a damned goldfish !
Rimbaud lets me be a.....

MOTHER
You'll always be my baby no matter wha.....

VERLAINE
I'M NOT YOUR DAMN BABY !
I'M TWENTY-EIGHT DAMNED YEARS OF BLOODY AGE WOMAN !
NOW GIVE ME THE FUCKING MONEY OR I SWEAR TO CHRIST
I'LL SWING FOR YOU !

MOTHER
Your language Paul
In front of your little broth....

VERLAINE
DON'T 'PAUL' ME WITCH !!
WHERE'S THE MONEY ? WHERE'S THE MONEY ?

[There may have been an undercurrent of
impending rape in the foregoing scene.
VERLAINE throws himself murderously
upon her now as the front doorbell
rings loud and long.]

MOTHER
Mathilde ! Mathilde !

VERLAINE
Mama ! Mama ! Don't leave me alone Mama !

MOTHER
I'm all right ! I'm all right now
Let me handle him
Just give me a moment with him...
....
There there there...my baby my baby... [Crooning over him]
Dansons la gigue
Dansons la gigue.....

[RIMBAUD roaming the back streets of Paris
in the early hours.]

RIMBAUD [sings]

Your love is sin your song a whine
SMASH UP THE MOULD !
Your mate a sow your child a wolf
Your prayer a scream your god a whore
SMASH UP THE MOULD !
Your prick is death your cunt decay
Climb in the grave the future's mine
SMASH UP THE MOULD !
AXE TO THE ROOT ! AXE TO THE ROOT !

FIFI

Short time mister ?

RIMBAUD

AXE TO THE ROOT !

FIFI

Come inside for a fiddle of fun
With one of me ten topless bottomless beauty-of-Bath belles of yer balls !
Come in and have a gan......
Oh it's only you

RIMAUD

Invent new loves create new words
BECOMING GOD !
Invent new flowers new colours sounds
Invent new smells sensations noise
BECOMING GOD !
Invent caresses futures dreams
Invent new sexes fears and joys
BECOMING GOD !
I'M FUCKING GOD !
I'M FUCKING GOD !

FIFI
Does your mother now you're out on the street this time of night sonny ?

RIMBAUD
I'M FUCKING GOD !

FIFI
Start none of them shinanigans here or I'll see you
Slung out of this street swifter than shit from a shovel !

RIMBAUD
Sex must be re-invented !

FIFI
Ah god love you
Can you still not get it up ?

RIMBAUD
I'm going to re-invent you Fifi

FIFI
Five francs and you can do anything you want to me

RIMBAUD
Today I invented a new vowel of the colour 'grellow'

FIFI
It's not important

RIMBAUD
Pardon ?

FIFI
Fucking

RIMBAUD
It is to me
I fuck cats

FIFI
About ten times a night for the past t...
God !

RIMBAUD
Every night ?

FIFI
It's hard to take it serious any more

RIMBAU
I fuck anything

FIFI
Two francs ?

RIMBAUD
I don't remember what two francs looks like

FIFI
....
Smoke ?

RIMBAUD
....
That's not tobacco

FIFI
How's M. Verlaine then ?

RIMBAUD
How's your bourgeois bollocks ?

FIFI
I like him
He's a good client
...
I like you... when I'm not working

RIMBAUD
I like you when you're not working

FIFI
You're soft... about the body
You don't work

RIMBAUD
I'm a magician

FIFI
Never been with a woman have you ?

RIMBAUD
Women...men...I told you...everything
I like dogs best

FIFI
Male or female ?

[FIFI goes down on all fours
playing the bitch-in-heat.
SHE comes at him seductively
whining and barking.
RIMBAUD amused then
disturbed then frankly frightened.]

RIMBAUD
STOP IT ! STOP IT !

FIFI
It's only a bit of fun
....
Ssh...shush... there now...

RIMBAUD
I'm not God
I'm not even a magician

FIFI
Doesn't matter to me
......
If you were mine...
I'd buy you a little farm somewhere down the country
Provence maybe

RIMBAUD
I have this puritan mother down the country
I promised Verlaine I'd go back and cut her throat
I clean forgot

FIFI
I have the money

RIMBAUD
Money is shit

FIFI
You want to know what I'm going to do with the money ?

RIMBAUD
No

FIFI
See them teeth ?

RIMBAUD
No

FIFI
I have only one dream
It's all about them teeth

RIMBAUD
You have good teeth...for a whore

FIFI
I look after myself
Do you want to hear my dream for the teeth ?

RIMBAUD
I said I don't

FIFI
I'm getting all them good teeth pulled out
Every last one and...
All my life I've dreamt this dream
That every tooth in my head is solid gold !
22 Carat !
Teeth !
A king's ransom in my mouth !
And then I wouldn't smile
Not for just anyone
But when I do
It's like a mad explosion of sunshine in the middle of the night
Flashing rich and bright and clean
Blinding them and making them feel ashamed that they aren't me
With that golden sun in my mouth
....
One of these nights
Maybe tonight
'Click !'
I'm going to turn the key in that door
Walk away
Like a golden snake from my dirty old skin
Walking away to my golden day

RIMBAUD
I could do that
Walk away from everything
If I wanted to

FIFI
If you were with me I'd make you strong
Working with them hands till they were hard and ...hard

RIMBAUD
I fought god at his own game

FIFI
What's your name ?

RIMBAUD
Rimbe

FIIFI
Rimbe
I think you are strong
You will have your golden day

RIMBAUD
I can make gold ! I'm a sorcerer ! Ha ha ha ha!

FIFI [sings]
Laughing men and women in their rage
He will have his love his here and now
Here without your sin now sans my grace...

RIMBAUD and FIFI [sing]
He will have his day
He will have his beauteous day
His love
His breath
His body
His day

Love and rage he will not go away
He will have his laugh his here and now
His alpha ending here omega now
He will have his day
He will have his beauteous day
His love
His breath
His body
His day

PART FOUR

'GREEN'

[RIMBAUD squatting on the street near MOTHER's house. VERLAINE hurries by.]

RIMBAUD
What's the hurry bastard ?

VERLAINE
Oh...Rimbaud....hello

RIMBAUD
What ever happened 'Rimbe' ? 'I love you Rimbe !' 'Don't leave me Rimbe !' ?

VERLAINE
How are you Rimbe ?

RIMBAUD
Do you not think you have some responsibility to me...to my work ?

VERLAINE
You sent me back to my mother
You know how my family swallows me once I cross that door

RIMBAUD
I know how Christ felt in Gethsemene

VERLAINE
I worry about you all the time

RIMBAUD
You won't have to worry about me much longer

VERLAINE
You have a job ? That's goo...

RIMBAUD
Job ? JOB ? What do you take me for ? I m the only poet in France !
Job ?
You want me to sweep the streets for your mother and her pack of fucking jackals ?
You want me to shovel the dogshit off their nice bourgeois streets for them ?

VERLAINE
Are you eating ?

RIMBAUD
How the hell could I be eating ?
Go on.... go about your business

VERLAINE
You obviously came up this way to see me

RIMBAUD
I came up here selling my arse
So I can pay the rent on that shithole you dumped me in

VERLAINE
I said I'd pay the rent

RIMBAUD
I pulled out of it a couple of hours back

VERLAINE
......
You might at least tell me where you'll be

RIMBAUD
If I knew you're the last person I'd tell

VERLAINE
Look... I have to run to the pharmacy for my wife's medicine
She hasn't been at all well...

RIMBAUD
Aw... that's too bad
Keeping Old Glory under wraps is she ? Hah !

VERLAINE
Actually yes
She hasn't a lot of energy

RIMBAUD
Well you needn't look at me with those sheep's eyes of yours
There's nothing to keep a poet in this slagheap

VERLAINE
Come down to the café...

RIMBAUD
Finished

VERLAINE
Just one

RIMBAUD
Too late

VERLAINE
I need to talk... to work with you

RIMBAUD
You betrayed me
I came for the blood-money Judas

VERLAINE
I have money
....

[RIMBAUD shoves his hand out for money]

The Café Cluny

......

[RIMBAUD shoves his hand out for money. VERLAINE takes money from various pockets and stuffs it in the other's hands.]

RIMBAUD
What do you have to do to get all this ?

VERLAINE
I'll just keep enough for the medicine

RIMBAUD
You still want to be a poet ?

VERLAINE
I have no choice

RIMBAUD
Come away from France with me

VERLAINE
Yes

RIMBAUD
Now

VERLAINE
Tomorrow

RIMBAUD
I'm leaving now

VERLAINE
The pharmacy

RIMBAUD
To hell with the pharmacy !

VERLAINE
The medicine is ready for.....

RIMBAUD
To hell with the medicine !

VERLAINE
My poor young wife...

RIMBAUD
To hell with your wife !

VERLAINE
This evening

RIMBAUD
Lickspittle !

VERLAINE
I'll follow you...

RIMBAUD [leaving]
Don't !

VERLAINE
Rimbe ! Rimbe ! I'm coming with you now !

RIMBAUD
The medicine...

VERLAINE
To hell with the medicine !

RIMBAUD
Your poor young wife, Verlaine

VERLAINE
To hell... TO HELL WITH MY WIFE ! Ha ha ha !

[EXEUNT laughing.
IMPROVISED SCENE;
the two poets in euphoric mood as
they revel in each other's company.]

RIMBAUD

'Eternal occurrence, tremblings of gods
under verduous seas, calm of animals
scattered over lush grazing, calm of
furrows ploughed in the great foreheads of
sorcerers...'

FIFI

'Cycles , vibrements divins des mers
verides, paix aux patis, semes d'animaux
Paix des rides que l'alchemie imprime aux
grades frontes studieux....'

RIMBAUD

.....

.....

When we first came to this city, I thought
I had truly taken you to Hell
'The feast of the Seven Sins is here...'

VERLAINE

'The most beauteous of the fallen angels
Is just sixteen. Beneath his garland of flowers
Arms crossed on garment's hem and throat
He dreams, eyes full of fire and tears...'

RIMBAUD

'In the end, O happiness, O reason, I stole
from the blue that is black, and lived
like the gold of pure light !'

VERLAINE

It is ours again

RIMBAUD
What ?

VERLAINE
Eternity
It is the sea fucking the sun !

[The POETS come down to earth.]

RIMBAUD
'Through me shall Hell make sacrifice to universal love...' Remember ?
....
For a while I was arrogant enough to believe we had actually done that

VERLAINE
We did

RIMBAUD
Drugs...booze...women...men... that was all you not me
Can you believe me when I say that every moment has been an....

VERLAINE
Ecstasy

RIMBAUD
An agony a flagellation
Debauchery is utterly repellent to me

VERLAINE
It's your second nature...your first

RIMBAUD
'I dreamed of crusades, unheard-of
explorations, revolutions in morals...I
I believed in every kind of witchcraft. I
I convinced myself I had created things: new
flowers. I thought I was God. I invented
the colour of vowels ! A black, E white, I
red, U green, O blue. I regulated the form

and movement of every consonant... I flattered myself with inventing a poetic language accessible to all the senses. I reserved translation rights. I wrote out silences and the nights. I recorded the inexpressible. I described frenzies... Oh dear Satan, you asked too much of me !'

VERLAINE
I no longer fear Hell

RIMBAUD
My puritan mother you see had done her work
Better than she or I knew.
I had been shot through the heart by Grace
Know what I was ?

VERLAINE
Poet...poet

RIMBAUD
'A drunken midge in a pub urinal, enamoured of pissed beer...dissolved by a single sunbeam'

VERLAINE
I'm not afraid of happiness

RIMBAUD
Or self-deception ?

VERLAINE
I understand

RIMBAUD
Don't count on my staying with you

VERLAINE
You're trying to start a row

RIMBAUD
A single sunbeam

VERLAINE
My mother teaches the piano...she has some wonderful young pupils
There's one little fellow of ten or eleven, Debussey,
Wanted to put music to the music of my work
It seems to tie in with your idea of the equivalences....

[MOTHER singing Verlaine's GREEN.
There are versions by Debussey and Fauré.]

RIMBAUD
It's like the day you suddenly realise the Winter is over

MOTHER [sings]
'Voici des fruits, des fleures, des feuilles et des branches,
Et puis, voici mon coeur, qui ne bat que pur vous,
Ne le dechirez pas avec vos deux mains blanches,
Et qu'a vos yeaux si beaux l'umble present soit doux...'

RIMBAUD
I shall break everything that stands between me and God !
I have never sinned you know
Everything I've ever done has been nothing more or less
Than a search for salvation !

VERLAINE
'On your young breast let my head roll
Sonorous with the clamour of your last kiss
Let that sweet storm subside so
That I sleep a little and you rest...'

RIMBAUD
Go back to your family Paul

VERLAINE
Don't start getting destructive

RIMBAUD
It may seem bizarre... that I should suddenly leave you
After all we've been through...

VERLAINE
I'm not playing this game with you

RIMBAUD
...When you'll no longer feel my arm under your neck
My breast to lie upon
Nor my lips upon your eyes...

VERLAINE
I know exactly what you're trying to do to me

RIMBAUD
...Because one day I shall have to go away
Very far away to help others...that's my destiny
It's no choice of mine dear heart

VERLAINE
DON'T LEAVE ME RIMBE ! DON'T LEAVE ME !

RIMBAUD
Eventually I must

VERLAINE
It's cruel and evil !
You've made me utterly dependant on you... your love...your body
Why can't you be content ?

RIMBAUD
I'm not blaming you for anything

VERLAINE
Blaming me !

RIMBAUD
Have you any idea of the courage it takes to admit

That my whole life has been a waste of time ?

VERLAINE
You're eighteen

RIMBAUD
I'm nineteen

VERLAINE
I don't think so
Eighteen or nineteen
You're the greatest French poet since Racine

RIMBAUD
Frankly that means nothing to me

VERLAINE
Look what you've done for me
A bourgeois fart
You've at least made me into a real artist
You...

RIMBAUD
All I ever wanted to do was to find God

VERLAINE
A few days ago you were shouting from the hilltops
We had become gods

RIMBAUD
No one can say I didn't try
I tried....as Baudelaire tried
'To plunge to the bottom of the abyss...
To Hell or Heaven what matter !
But in the depths of the Unknown to find the new !

VERLAINE
We found it !

RIMBAUD
You know who speaks through my most profound poetry ?

VERLAINE
God

RIMBAUD
A bloody child ! Me. Me and my stupid
mother and my snotty-nosed sister and my coward
of a teacher of Classics with his snout
reeking of the pigswill feeding-trough of
the education system ! That's what I
dragged up from my season in Hell ! There
was no one in my abyss only me ! God
wasn't bloody there ! I was down the wrong hole
I was up the wrong tower !

VERLAINE
You have fifty years' writing ahead of you

RIMBAUD
I'M FINISHED WITH IT ! CAPUT !
.....
.....
I know what I have to do with the rest of my life
Something purely physical

VERLAINE
Your mission is metaphysical

RIMBAUD
I did it in good faith

VERLAINE
Of course you did

RIMBAUD
But should I go back to poetry now
It would be a terrible sin

Now that I know

VERLAINE
You don't leave poetry

RIMBAUD
I am capable of any sacrifice

VERLAINE
If you do it I'll do it

RIMBAUD
You are part of what I must leave behind

VERLAINE
This is your old sadistic jealousy

RIMBAUD
You above all should understand my spirituality

VERLAINE
You've fallen for another tramp
That's it isn't it ?

RIMBAUD
Paul will you give me the money to make a start somewhere
In the sun ?

VERLAINE
In the sun is it ?
The two of us ?

RIMBAUD
Me

VERLAINE
So who is the lucky man this time ?
Or is it a woman ?
Not a dog ?

RIMBAUD
If you love me you'll do this last kindness for me

VERLAINE
Kindness
If you try to ditch me
I swear to Christ I'll do for the both of us !

RIMBAUD
You'll find your own salvation

VERLAINE
You know fucking well where my salvation lies
In a sadistic perverted child
Who can't bear to see himself or anyone else happy !
You should be locked away Rimbaud !

RIMBAUD
Stop your whining you'd sicken a saint

VERLAINE
Swear you won't abandon me

RIMBAUD
I am leaving you

VERLAINE
....
May I ask when precisely ?

RIMBAUD
Now
I could wait till tomorrow if the money will take time

VERLAINE
God you are despicable

RIMBAUD
I'd need about three hundred francs

VERLAINE
Two francs
I'll give you two francs every day you stay with me

RIMBAUD
Don't play your mother's game with me

VERLAINE
Promise you won't leave me and I'll give you every sou I've got

RIMBAUD
I can't lie to you Paul
You're my best friend

VERLAINE
An hour ago we were as happy as...

RIMBAUD
A million years ago

VERLAINE
I followed you to Hell

RIMBAUD
That was your affair

VERLAINE
And if I kill myself ?

RIMBAUD
None of my business

VERLAINE
And if I kill you ?

RIMBAUD

.............[shrugs]

VERLAINE

....

I expect I have to believe you're serious

RIMBAUD

Verlaine even as we speak
I see my life open up before me like a picture
Labour...hard manual labour...abroad
I think Africa is right for me
I shall build roads and bridges and reservoirs
My body will become hard as tempered steel
My skin burned black in the desert sun...

VERLAINE

And Art ?

RIMBAUD

I shall find God
At the bottom of a stone-quarry...at the end of a railway line
The last place you could imagine

VERLAINE

And no place for me ?

RIMBAUD

No place for you

VERLAINE

Well that's all very neat and tidy
I don't believe one damn word of it needless to say
But it does seem clear you want rid of me...and I...
I love you enough to co-operate
At least to the extent of doing away with myself

RIMBAUD

I never wished that on you

VERLAINE
It's a cliché of course for which I apologise
But truly I could not live without you
Being with you is as vital as breath itself

RIMBAUD
....
......

VERLAINE
Is that it then ?

RIMBAUD
It seems so Paul

[VERLAINE fetches a revolver and bullets.
He loads the gun.]

VERLAINE
I'll ask once more
Are still saying everything is finished between us ?

RIMBAUD
Yes

VERLAINE
I'll go and say goodbye to my mother and...
And to my wife and child....
If they'll see me
You know she's been through the Courts and got a separation
On the strength of my relationship with you ?
Of course you do
So I've burnt my bridges haven't I ?

PART FIVE

'BLUE' ['GOLD']

[Emotional reunion between MOTHER and VERLAINE. Debussey's *Clair De Lune* plays through this scene in a piano solo.]

VERLAINE
She didn't even answer one of my letters

MOTHER
She wouldn't open them

VERLAINE
I must see her
And the wee boy...how is he ?

MOTHER
Fine
The Court...you're forbidden by the Court to see either of them
Those lawyers said such terrible things about you
You and that creature....
I hope you've left him for good this time

VERLAINE
Did you tell her I'm putting an end to myself ?

MOTHER
Aw don't say that baby
Paul you know drink doesn't agree with you

VERLAINE
Did you tell her ?

MOTHER
I told her

VERLAINE
Well ? Has she relented about seeing me before I shoot myself ?

MOTHER
She was quite rude about that
Not at all like Mathilde
Such a passive girl
Remember the time you tried to burn her hair ?
She just sat staring at you

VERLAINE
None of you gives a damn if I live or die

MOTHER
My sons are all I ha....

VERLAINE
Mother ! I'm your only son !
That...that thing is just a... a human pickle !

MOTHE
Don't be unkind to your brother Paul

VERLAINE
I've watched you nursing that blob in a bottle for twenty years

MOTHER
He'll be sixteen on the Feast of The Annunciation: 25th of March

VERLAINE
Everyone thinks you have a slate loose

MOTHER
I stand by my sons

VERLAINE
Son

MOTHER
Sons

VERLAINE
It gives me the creeps
There's something unnatural about keeping a...

MOTHER
Unnatural ! That's a good one ! 'Unnatural' !

VEERLAINE
We're the laughing-stock of Paris !

MOTHER
Unnatural ! That's exactly the word the judge used about you and that... that pervert
Rumple or whatever you call him

VERLAINE
Rimbaud

MOTHER
Rumple
'Unnatural and unspeakable' he said

VERLAINE
Rimbaud ! Rimbaud !
You get it right because you're going to hear it from me for the rest of your days
And mine
However short they may be

[Again there will be the suggestion of rape in the following.]

MOTHER
Paul ! Paul ! You're hurting me !

VERLAINE
Say it...Rimbaud !

MOTHER
Rimbaud
Let me go...please

VERLAINE
Rimbaud is going to Africa and I'm going with him
We need three hundred francs !

MOTHE
I haven't got three hundred francs ! Aaagh ! Stop...please stop !

VERLAINE
Three hundred francs !

MOTHER
I'll get it for you

VERLAINE
Now ?

MOTHER
Now...now !

VERLAINE
Three hundred francs !

MOTHER
You'll ruin me

VERLAINE
Three hundred francs !

MOTHER
This money was for your brother's education...

VERLAINE
And get that obscenity out of the house or I'll bloody do it for you !

MOTHER
You dare lay a finger on my son and I'll...

[THEY struggle for the foetus.
VERLAINE gets it.]

VERLAINE
Sixteen is he ?
Let's see if he can walk down the fucking stairs if he's sixteen !

[VERLAINE hurls the foetus
down the stairs. MOTHER screaming.
Sound of breaking glass, children
squealing and running down stairs.]

MOTHER
MURDERER !!!

[VERLAINE and RIMBAUD.
VERLAINE with the gun.]

VERLAINE
I got the money

RIMBAUD
I'm glad you changed your mind about blowing your brains out

VERLAINE
I haven't changed my mind about anything
Have you ?

RIMBAUD
No
....
I got your telegram about joining the Carlists in Spain...that's why I stayed

It's a good idea

VERLAINE
They rejected me

RIMBAUD
Oh dear
They mustn't have heard about your heroics in the commune
Was the housemaid volunteering with you ?

VERLAINE
I have the money for Africa

RIMBAUD
Oh...that's really good of you Paul
I'll pay it back when I get on my feet

VERLAINE
I'm going with you

RIMBAUD
Uh-huh

VERLAINE
I'll give up poetry...I'll work with you...dig ditches.... anything !

RIMBAUD
I don't want to talk any more about it

VERLAIANE
Kiss me Rimbe !

RIMBAUD
Don't

VERLAINE
Hold me a second !

RIMBAUD

....

Come !

....

That's enough ! That's it ! It's finished !

VERLAINE

It's not finished ! I know what you feel !

RIMBAUD

FUCK OFF OF ME !

VERLAINE

I HAVE TO BE WITH YOU ! YOU KNOW THAT !

RIMBAUD

Money !

VERLAINE

No money if I don't go with you

RIMBAUD

.....

Lend me fifty

VERLAINE

All or nothing

RIMBAUD

Come on Paul !

Money for Rimbe !

VERLAINE

We go together or we die together !

There is no life no future without you !

RIMBAUD

Just fifty

VERLAINE
Uh-huh

RIMBAUD
....
Then I'll have to go without money

VERLAINE
Take me with you Rimbaud for pity's sake take me with you

[RIMBAUD walks past him and is leaving without looking back.]

There'll be terrible trouble if you don't come back right now Rimbaud !

RIMBAUD
Well ?

VERLAINE
Last time

RIMBAUD
Money

VERLAINE
Take me

RIMBAUD
No Paul

[VERLAINE shoots him.]

VERLAINE
I love you Rimbe !

RIMBAUD
You're fucking crazy!

VERLAINE
I cannot live or write or let you live unless we are together !

[VERLAINE shoots him again.
RIMBAUD falls... scrambles
somehow out of the room.
POLICE WHISTLES.

LIGHT CHANGE.

[VERLAINE, manacled, in a heap
on the floor of a prison cell.
MOTHER elsewhere nursing a tiny coffin.
RIMBAUD leaving the country.
FIFI watching him.]

VERLAINE
Oh sweet suffering Jesus don't desert me !
Not prison ! I can't rot two years in a filthy prison cell ! I can't !
I'll never sin again ! Forgive me Lord Jesus I love !
I am a poet ! I shall die if they take my freedom from me !
Aaaaaaaggghhh !!

RIMBAUD
'His day ! The abolition of all loud and agitated suffering in more intense music.
His footsteps ! Migrations vaster than ancient invasions. O he and us!
Self-esteem kinder than lost charities.
O world ! And the clear song of new woes ! He knew and loved us all.
Let us, this winter night, from cape to cape, from pole to chateau,
from throng to the beach, from look to look,
strength and emotion drained, hail see and send him away, and under seas and on the heights of snow deserts,
follow his glances, his breath, his body, his day...'

FIFI [following Rimbaud]
....his glances, his breath, his body, his day...

VERLAINE
I AM ENTOMBED !!!

RIMBAUD and FIFI [sing]
Laughing men and women in their rage
He will have his love his here and now
Here without your sin now sans your grace
He will have his day
He will have his beauteous day
His love
His breath,
His body
His day

Love and rage he will not go away
He will have his laugh his here and now
Alpha ending here omega now
He will have his beauteous day
His love
His breath,
His body
His day

[VERLAINE prostrate and quite still. His attention is finally attracted to sunlight through a small window high in his prison cell. For a few moments he drinks it in, then 'composes' LE CIEL .]

VERLAINE
'The sky is, above the roof,
So blue, so calm,
A palm, above the roof,
Cradles the wind.

Soft calls the bell
In the sky I see.
Love-call of the bird
In the tree I see.
My God, my God, life is there,
Quiet, uncluttered.
That drowsy murmur there

Comes from the town.

....What have you done, you
Who weep eternal tears ?
Tell me what you have done, you,
With your youth ?'

END OF THE PLAY

www.ingramcontent.com/pod-product-compliance
Ingram Content Group UK Ltd.
Pitfield, Milton Keynes, MK11 3LW, UK
UKHW012242240726
13966UKWH00003B/1250

9 781847 538888